PEANUT
BUTTER
&
CUPCAKE!

PEANUT BUTTER & CUPCAKE!

Terry Border

Philomel Books • An imprint of Penguin Group (USA)

Philomel Books

Published by the Penguin Group
Penguin Group (USA) LLC
375 Hudson Street, New York, NY 10014

USA | Canada | UK | Ireland | Australia | New Zealand | India | South Africa | China
penguin.com
A Penguin Random House Company

Library of Congress Cataloging-in-Publication Data
Border, Terry, 1965–
Peanut Butter & Cupcake / Terry Border.   pages cm
Summary: Peanut Butter sets out with his soccer ball to find a friend after moving to a new town, but everyone from Hamburger to Soup seems to be too busy to play.   [1. Friendship—Fiction. 2. Moving, Household—Fiction. 3. Food—Fiction.] I. Title. II. Title: Peanut Butter and Cupcake.
PZ7.B64832Pe 2014   [E]—dc23   2013039974
Manufactured in China by South China Printing Co. Ltd.
ISBN 978-0-399-16773-7
1 3 5 7 9 10 8 6 4 2
Edited by Jill Santopolo.   Design by Semadar Megged.   Text set in 21.5-point Hank BT.
The art was done by manipulating and photographing three-dimensional objects.

To my best friend, Judi

Peanut Butter got a ball for his birthday. He was kind of bad at kicking it with his feet, but was kind of good at balancing it on his head.

Still, it wasn't much fun playing
with a ball all by himself.

"Want to play with me?" he asked his mom.
They had just moved to town and Peanut
Butter didn't have any friends yet.

"I think you should go outside and find someone to be your new friend," she answered.

Peanut Butter liked that idea
very much, so off he went.

It wasn't long before
he saw a someone.

"Hello, I'm new here, and I'd like to play
Maybe now, maybe later—or even all day
I'll make you chuckle deep down in your belly
And we'll go together like Peanut Butter and . . .

Hamburger!"

"I'm sorry," said Hamburger, "but I'm busy walking the dogs. Thanks for asking, though."

"You're welcome," said Peanut Butter. "Maybe next time." And he kept walking.

Then he saw Cupcake, playing by herself. He thought
she looked sweet, and might make a good friend.
"Hello, I'm new here, and I'd like to play
Maybe now, maybe later—or even all day
I'll make you chuckle deep down in your belly
And we'll go together like Peanut Butter and . . .

Cupcake!"

"I'm building sprinkle-castles," said Cupcake.
"You can stay and watch, but don't hit my castle with
your ball or I'll be mad!"

Peanut Butter didn't want to make anyone mad. "That's
okay," Peanut Butter said. And he kept walking.

Then he saw Egg rolling down the path.
"Hello, I'm new here, and I'd like to play
Maybe now, maybe later—or even all day
I'll make you chuckle deep down in your belly
And we'll go together like Peanut Butter and . . .

                                              Egg!"

"Peanut Butter and Egg? That's funny. You're
cracking me up!" Egg laughed.
And then he really did crack.

                    Peanut Butter didn't want the egg to
                    laugh any more. So he kept walking.

He found someone jumping.
"Hello, I'm new here, and I'd like to play
Maybe now, maybe later—or even all day
I'll make you chuckle deep down in your belly
And we'll go together like Peanut Butter and . . .

Meatball!"

"32 . . . 33 . . . 34 . . . Shh! I'm counting my jumps!" said Meatball. "35 . . . 36 . . . 37 . . . I'm trying to set a record!"

Peanut Butter whispered back, "But I have this ball, and—"

"38 . . . 39 . . . 40 . . . Shhh!" said Meatball.

Peanut Butter kept walking.
Finding a friend was harder than
he thought it was going to be.

Then Peanut Butter saw another someone sitting under a tree, and that was good because he was ready to sit down, too. Even though he was getting tired, he gave it another try.

"Hello, I'm new here, and I'd like to play
Maybe now, maybe later—or even all day
I'll make you chuckle deep down in your belly
And we'll go together like Peanut Butter and . . .

                                        French Fries!"

"Not right now," said French Fries.
"I just remembered I'm supposed to
help Hamburger with his hot dogs,
and I need to catch up!"

Peanut Butter walked up to
one more someone who was
practicing his ABCs.
But before he could open
his mouth . . .

Soup picked up a spoon, dipped it into himself,
and then showed it to Peanut Butter.
In the spoon were two letters, an "N" and an "O."

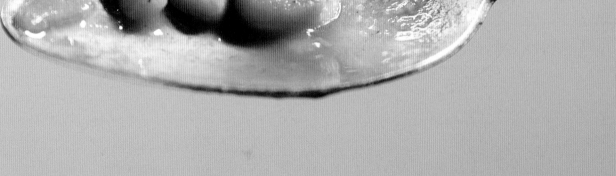

"But I didn't say anything yet,"
said Peanut Butter.
"You didn't have to," said Soup.
"Oh," said Peanut Butter.

Peanut Butter found a bench to sit on. He was almost ready to give up.

But as he sat there, so very sad, a new kid walked up to him.

"Hello," she said.
Peanut Butter took a deep breath.
"Um . . . Hello, I'm new here, and I'd like to play
Maybe now, maybe later—or even all day
I'll make you chuckle deep down in your belly
And we'll go together like Peanut Butter and . . .

. . . Jelly!"

"Sure. I'll be your friend," said Jelly. "But . . . could you teach me how to keep the ball on my head? I'm only good with my feet."

So they taught each other what they knew

and made each other chuckle deep down in their bellies.

It wasn't long before their laughing made the other kids come over. They asked if they could play, too. Of course, Peanut Butter and Jelly were happy to let them join in.

As his new friends knocked the ball around with their feet and their heads and, in one case, his buns, Peanut Butter chuckled deep down in his belly because they all went together like Peanut Butter and Hamburger and Cupcake and Egg and Meatball and French Fries and Soup and . . .

Jelly.

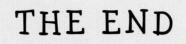